OTHER BOOKS FROM KANE/MILLER

One Woolly Wombat

The Magic Bubble Trip

The House From Morning to Night

Wilfrid Gordon McDonald Partridge

Brush

I Want My Potty

Girl From the Snow Country

Cat In Search of a Friend

The Truffle Hunter

Goodbye Rune

Winnie the Witch

The Umbrella Thief

The Park Bench

Sorry, Miss Folio!

Paul and Sebastian

First American Edition 1988 by Kane/Miller Book Publishers
Brooklyn, N.Y. & La Jolla, California

Orignally published in Spanish under the title *La Noche De Las Estrellas* by Ediciones Ekaré-Banco del Libro, Caracas, Venezuela. Copyright © 1987 Ediciones Ekaré-Banco del Libro.

Printed and bound in Italy by New Interlitho SPA Milan

2 3 4 5 6 7 8 9 10

Library of Congress Cataloging-in-Publication Data

Gutiérrez, Douglas.
[Noche de las estrellas. English]
The night of the stars / Douglas Gutiérrez, María Fernanda Oliver; translated by Carmen Diana Dearden. — 1st American ed.
p. cm.
Translation of: La noche de las estrellas.
"A Crankly Nell book."
Summary: A man who does not like the darkness of night finds a way to bring some light to it.
ISBN 0-916291-17-0 : $9.95
[1. Night—Fiction. 2. Stars—Fiction. 3. Moon—Fiction.]
I. Oliver. María Fernanda. II. Title.
PZ7.G9843Ni 1988
[E]—dc19 88-16900
CIP
AC

THE NIGHT OF THE STARS

Douglas Gutiérrez
María Fernanda Oliver

Translated by Carmen Diana Dearden

A CRANKY NELL BOOK

Kane/Miller Book Publishers

Brooklyn, New York & La Jolla, California

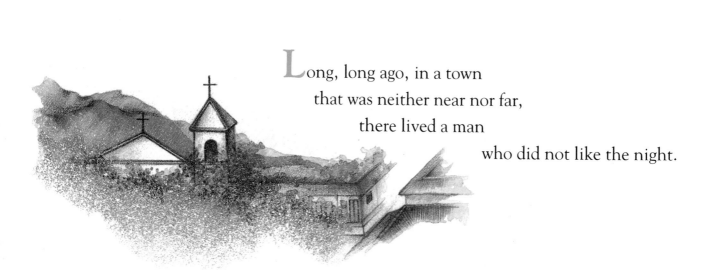

Long, long ago, in a town
that was neither near nor far,
there lived a man
who did not like the night.

During the day, in the sunlight,
he worked weaving baskets,
watching over his animals
and watering his vegetables.
Often he would sing.
But as soon as the sun set behind the mountain,
this man who did not like the night
would become sad, for his world suddenly
turned gray, dark and black.
"Night again! Horrible night!" he would cry out.

He would then pick up his baskets,
light his lamp
and shut himself up in his house.
Sometimes he would look out the window,
but there was nothing to see
in the dark sky. So he would put
out his lamp and go to bed.

One day, at sunset,
   the man went to the mountain.
   Night was beginning to cover the blue sky.
   The man climbed to the
highest peak and shouted:
            "Please, night. Stop!"

And the night did stop for a moment.

"What is it?" she asked in a soft deep voice.

"Night, I don't like you. When you come, the light goes away and the colors disappear. Only the darkness remains."

"You're right," answered the night. "It is so."

"Tell me, where do you take the light?" asked the man.

"It hides behind me, and I cannot do anything about it," replied the night. "I'm very sorry."

The night finished stretching and covered the world with darkness.

The man came down
from the mountain
and went to bed.

But, he could not sleep.

Nor, during the next day could he work.

All he could think about was

his conversation with the night.

And in the afternoon,

when the light began to disappear again,

he said to himself:

"I know what to do."

Once more
he went to the mountain.
The night was like an
immense awning, covering all things.
When at last he reached the
highest point on the mountain,
the man stood on his tiptoes,
and with his finger poked a hole
in the black sky.
A pinprick of light flickered through the hole.
The man who did not like the night was delighted.
He poked holes all over the sky. Here, there, everywhere,
and all over the sky
little points of light appeared.

Amazed now at what he could do,
the man made a fist
and punched it through the darkness.
A large hole opened up,
and a huge round light,
almost like a grapefruit, shone through.
All the escaping light cast a brilliant glow
at the base of the mountain
and lit up everything below . . .
the fields, the street, the houses.
Everything.

That night, no one in the town slept.

And ever since then,
the night is full of lights,
and people everywhere
can stay up late . . .
looking at the moon
and the stars.

GOOD MORNING!

TO ALL THE CUTE LITTLE FAMILIES
WHO TOLD ME THEY LOVED *THE GOODNIGHT BOOK*,
THIS IS FOR YOU.

Published in 2017 by Simply Read Books www.simplyreadbooks.com

Text & illustrations © 2017 Lori Joy Smith

Library and Archives Canada Cataloguing in Publication

Smith, Lori Joy, 1973-, author, illustrator
The good morning book / written and illustrated by Lori Joy Smith.

ISBN 978-1-77229-004-2 (bound)
I. Title.
PS8637.M56523G65 2016   jC813'.6   C2015-906573-9

We gratefully acknowledge for their financial support of our publishing program the Canada Council for the Arts, the BC Arts Council, and the Government of Canada through the Canada Book Fund (CBF).

Manufactured in Korea.
Book design by Sara Gillingham Studio.

10 9 8 7 6 5 4 3 2 1

LORI JOY SMITH

the GOOD MORNING BOOK

SIMPLY READ BOOKS

In English,
they say

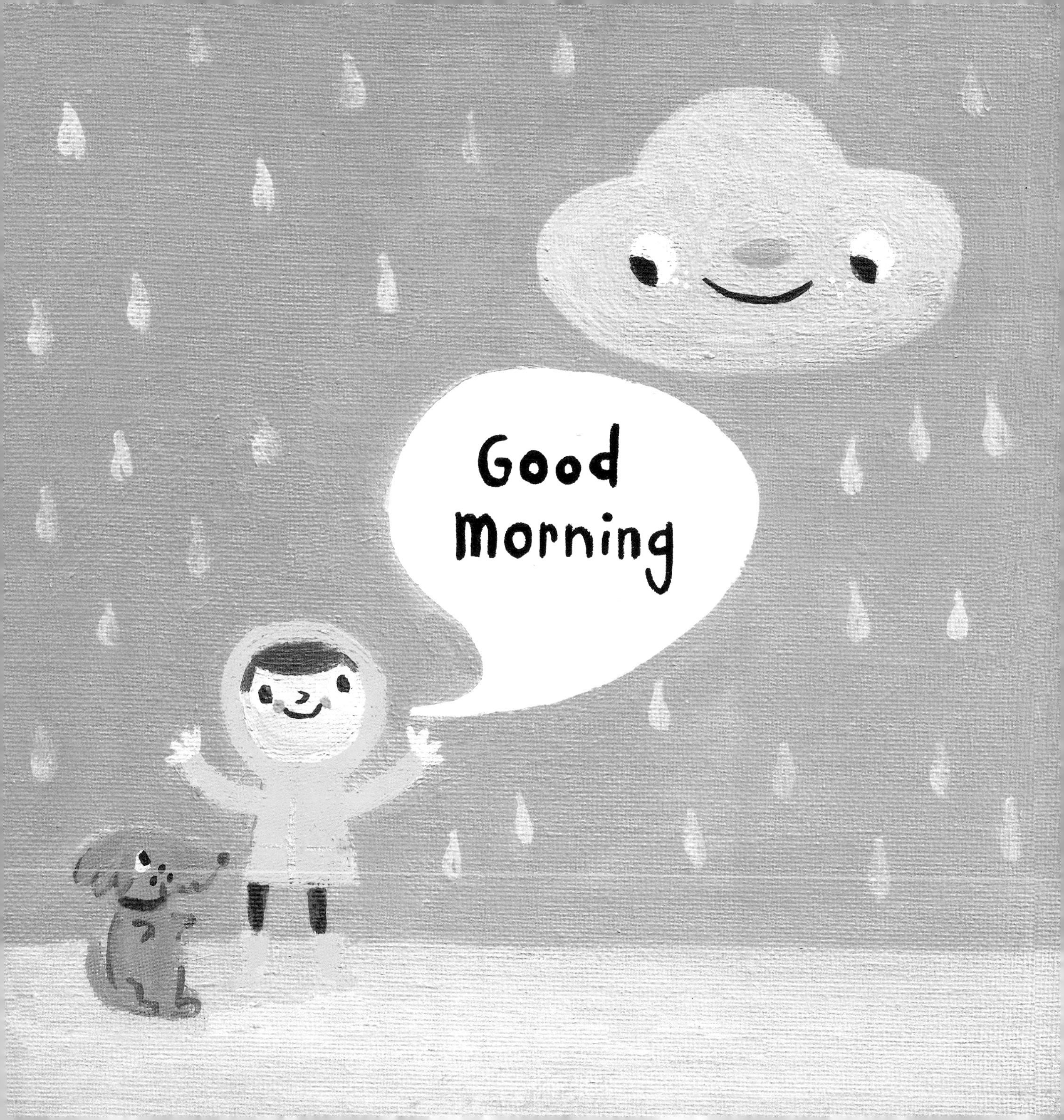
Good Morning

In Italian,
they say

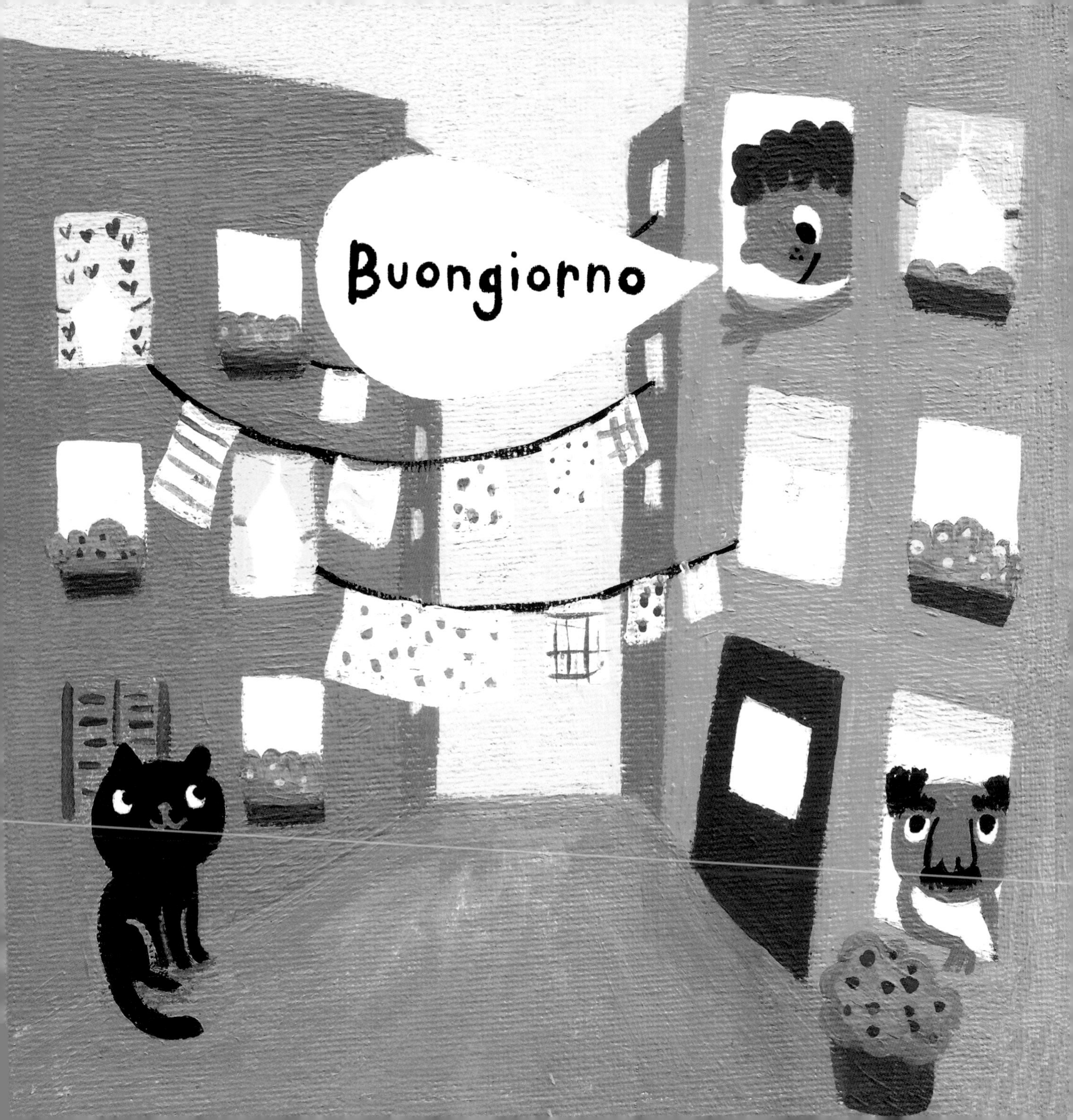
Buongiorno

In Japanese,
they say

But in some far off
places they say...

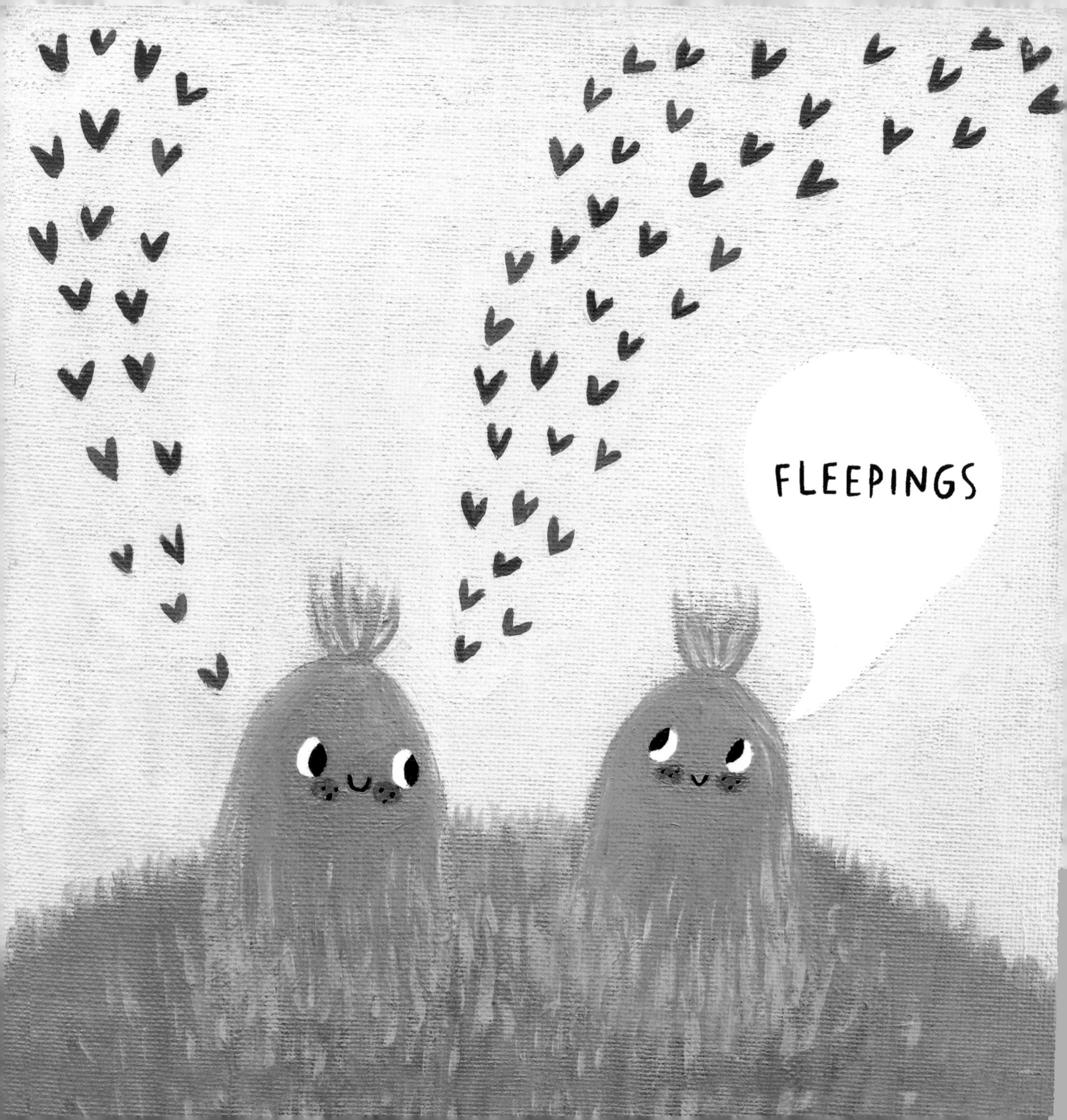
FLEEPINGS

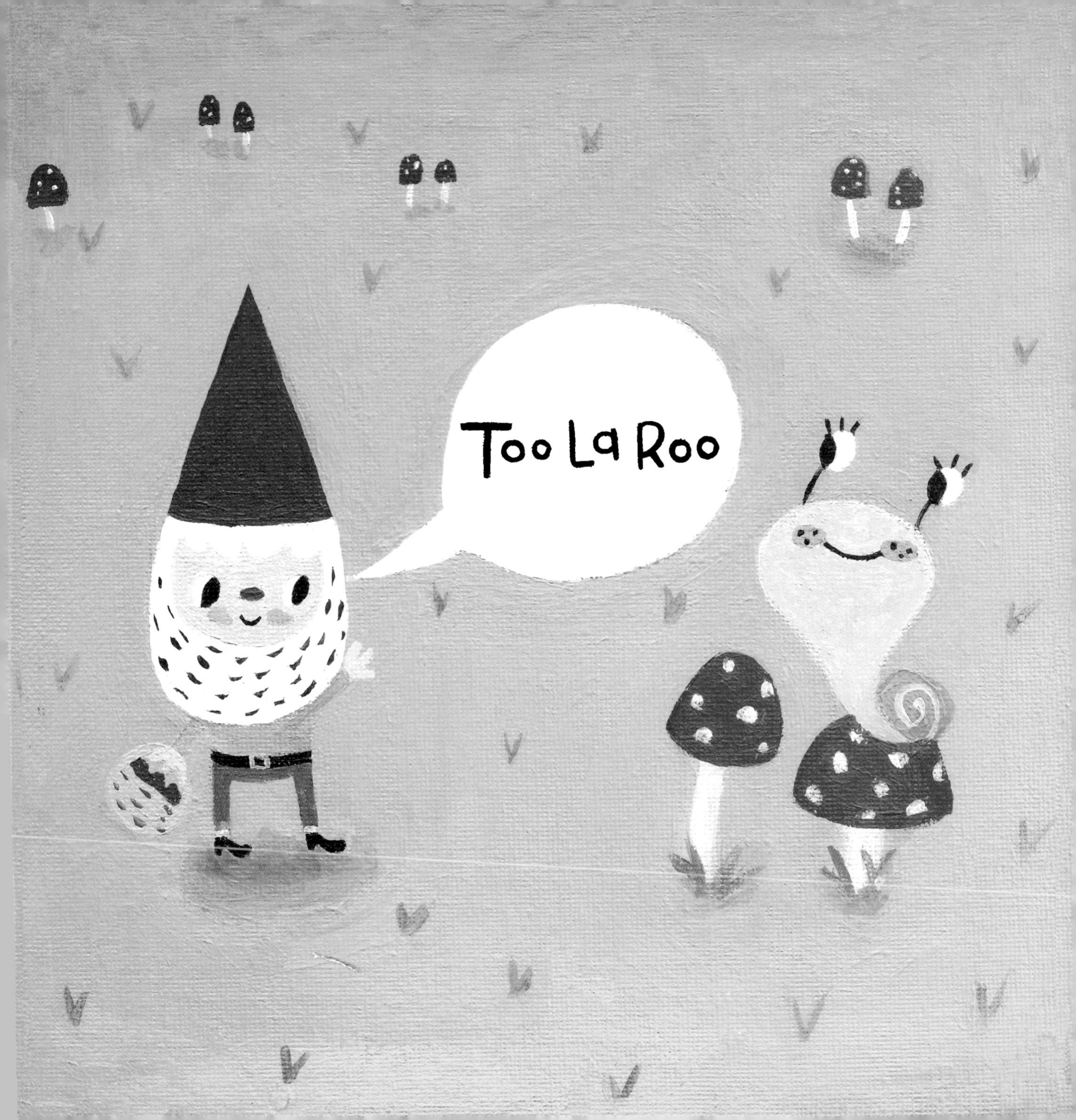
Too La Roo

How do YOU say GOOD MORNING ?